THIS WALKER BOOK BELONGS TO:

_____

_____

_____

For Holly
– D. C.

For Karina Anastasia
– S. M.

First edition published in Great Britain 2006 by Walker Books Ltd
87 Vauxhall Walk, London SE11 5HJ

10 9 8 7 6 5 4 3 2

Text © 2005 Doreen Cronin
Illustrations © 2005 Scott Menchin

This book has been typeset in Bliss

Printed in China

British Library Cataloguing in Publication Data:
a catalogue record for this book is available from the British Library

ISBN-13: 978-1-84428-210-4
ISBN-10: 1-84428-210-4

www.walkerbooks.co.uk

WALKER BOOKS
AND SUBSIDIARIES
LONDON · BOSTON · SYDNEY · AUCKLAND

Wiggle

doreen cronin

ART BY

SCOTT MENCHIN

Do you wake up wake up

with a wiggle?

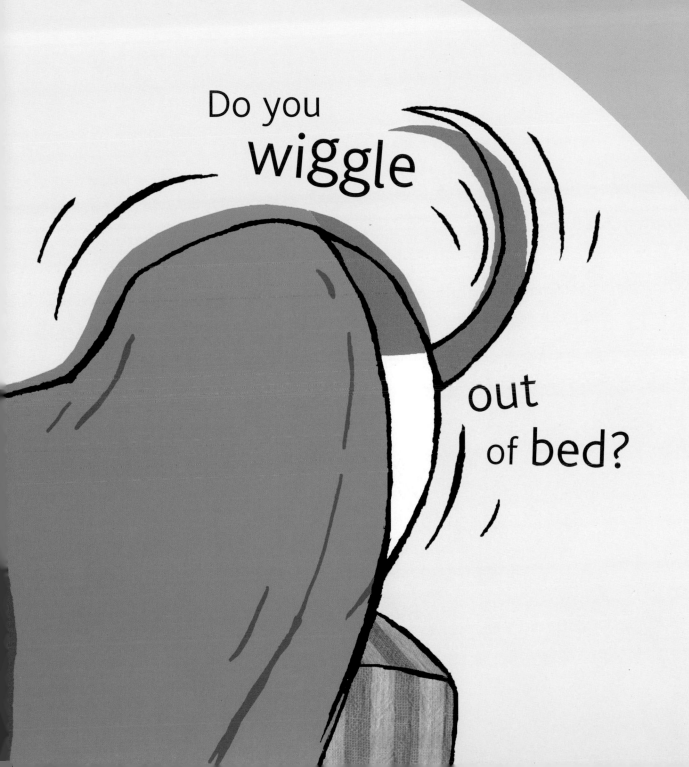

it might **end up** on your head.

First **wiggle** where your

tail would be.

Then
wiggle
all
your hair.

Feeling **extra** silly?

Can you
wiggle

with
your
shadow?

Can you **wiggle** with your toys?

When you **wiggle** with gorillas,

do they make a wiggle noise?

Can you
wiggle
in the
water?

Wiggle **one** fin on each side.

Or wiggle like a crocodile –

open
big
and
wide.

When
you
wiggle
where
your
wings
would be,

wiggles
fill the sky.

Wiggle **slowly** when with polar bears.

They're very wiggle shy.

Snakes are one big wiggle.

No wings.

No tails.

No feet.

Some wiggles are worth waiting for ...

Would you join me for a wiggle?

Would you **wiggle** on the **moon?**

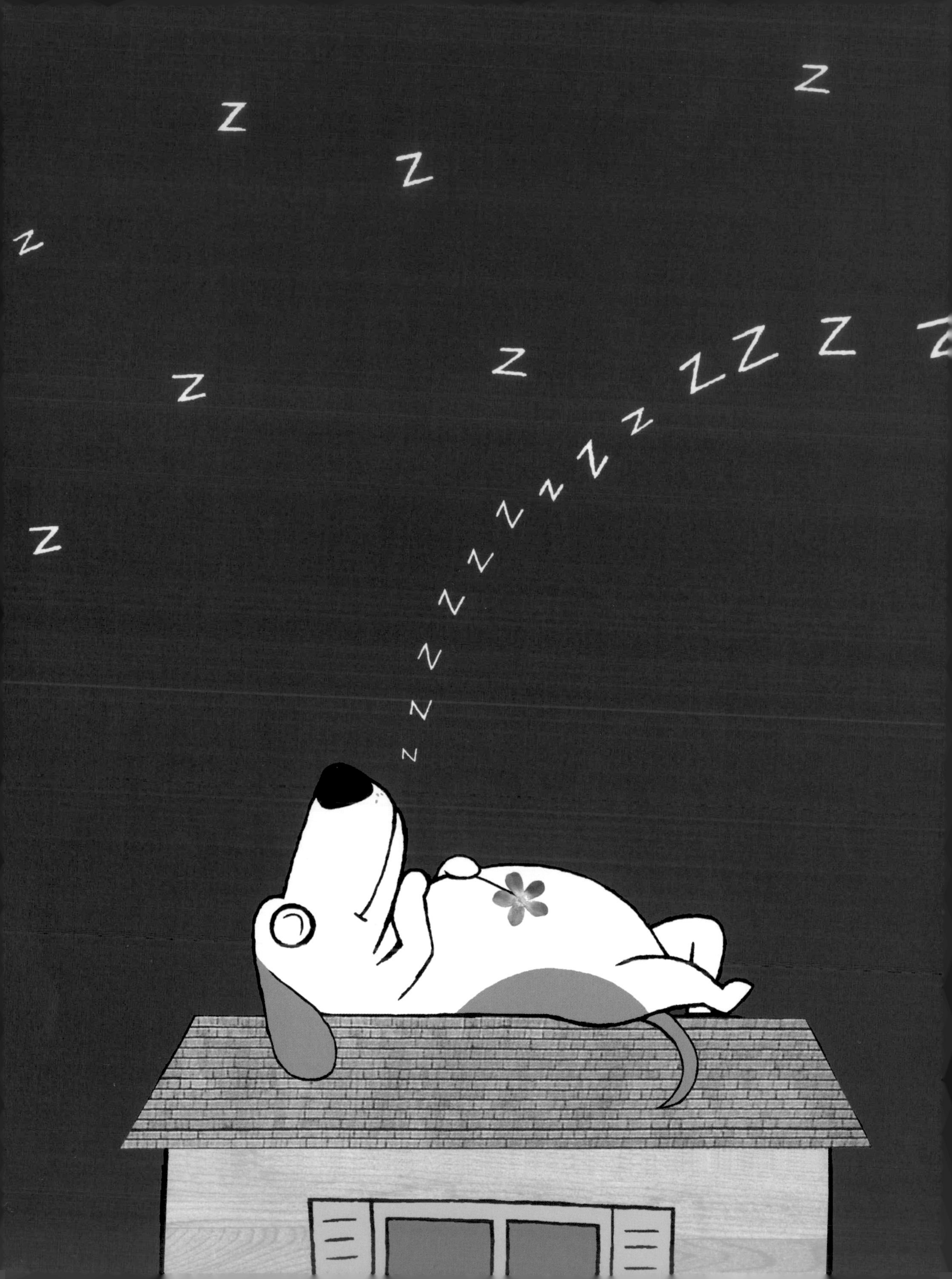

I think
we're out
of wiggles
now.
See you
wiggle
soon!

WALKER BOOKS is the world's leading
independent publisher of children's books.
Working with the best authors and illustrators
we create books for all ages, from babies
to teenagers – books your child will
grow up with and always remember. So…

FOR THE BEST CHILDREN'S BOOKS,
LOOK FOR THE BEAR